Cleanskin

Val McDermid

HarperCollins*Publishers*
77–85 Fulham Palace Road,
Hammersmith, London W6 8JB

www.harpercollins.co.uk

A paperback original 2006
4

A catalogue record for this book
is available from the British Library

ISBN: 978-0-00-721672-7

Set in Stone Serif by SX Composing DTP, Rayleigh, Essex

Printed and bound in Great Britain by
Clays Ltd, St Ives plc

Cleanskin

Val McDermid grew up in a Scottish mining community then read English at Oxford. She was a journalist for sixteen years, spending the last three years as Northern Bureau Chief of a national Sunday tabloid. She is now a full-time writer and divides her time between Cheshire and Northumberland.

Her novels have won international acclaim and a number of awards. *A Place of Execution* won both the Anthony Award for best novel and the *Los Angeles Times* 2001 Book of the Year Award Mystery/Thriller, while *The Mermaids Singing* took the 1995 Gold Dagger for best crime novel of the year.

CHAPTER ONE

WHEN A CHILD DIES, everybody hurts – family, friends and strangers alike. When a child is murdered, anger mixes with the pain. The only difference is that more strangers are drawn in. Doctors have to work out how it happened. Police officers have to figure out who is to blame. Reporters swarm all over the case like wasps round jam. Everybody takes it to heart.

That's how it was when Katie Farrell died. It was clear from the start that the fire that killed her was no accident. The firemen could smell the petrol as soon as they got there. Plus, the fire had started right outside her bedroom door, a place where no petrol should ever have been. The other people in the house that night escaped easily – her mother, her father and the Spanish girl who cooked their meals and took care of Katie when her parents weren't around. But not Katie. She didn't stand a chance.

My name is Andy Martin and I am a cop. I

heard about Katie Farrell's death in a phone call that woke me around two in the morning. I don't normally cover this sort of thing. My beat is serious crime and my team builds cases against serious villains – gangsters, people smugglers, drug dealers, big-time robbers. Scumbags, yes, but not normally the sort of scumbags who burn a nine-year-old girl to death in her own bedroom.

They called me because Katie Farrell wasn't just any nine-year-old girl. She was the daughter of Jack Farrell, and I was the world expert on Jack Farrell. Whenever his name hit any police computer, a big flag would go up saying, *Call Detective Chief Inspector Andy Martin*. Farrell had no criminal record, but that didn't mean he was an innocent man. Farrell's crew ran just about every dirty racket you could think of: drugs, guns, hookers, porn. You name it, they were into it. They bought and sold human lives like they were bargains on eBay. We'd been after Jack Farrell for years, but we'd never been able to lay a finger on him. He was still what we call a cleanskin – somebody who had no criminal record, meaning he had all the rights and freedoms available to decent citizens.

But I knew the truth. And I wanted Jack Farrell so bad I could taste it.

So of course they called me. Because Katie Farrell was dead. Dead in a way that said somebody was out to hit her father where it hurt most.

When I got down to Hampshire, Jack Farrell was standing barefoot outside a house about half the size of Wembley stadium. He was naked apart from boxer shorts and a blanket someone had thrown over his shoulders. He looked like he was the one who had died.

I saw two things that night I had never seen before. I saw a man whose beautiful life had been shattered with one blow. I also saw Jack Farrell's tattoos.

Others had described them to me – vivid colours, dramatic patterns, the finest examples of the skill of the tattoo artist. A dragon covered his torso, its tail disappearing into the waistband of his boxers, only to re-emerge on his left thigh. Every green scale was cleanly etched. A scarlet tongue of flame licked across the right side of his chest, climbing up to his shoulder. On one arm, I could see a samurai warrior, sword raised as if to attack the dragon. On the other arm, a beautiful woman covered her nakedness with hands and a long mane of red hair. It was a story without words, written on Jack Farrell's body.

It was also a story that he mostly kept hidden. In all the time I'd been watching Farrell, I'd never seen him in short sleeves. Unlike most villains, who display their tatts as if they were visible proof of how hard they are, Farrell's body art was kept private. I'd heard it said that he took his shirt off when he was about to kill in cold blood. The word on the street was that Jack Farrell's tatts were the last thing quite a few bad boys had seen in this world. It was yet another way of making sure he kept the opposition in fear.

But that night, Jack Farrell wouldn't have scared anybody. The fire had robbed him of more than his Katie. He was a hollow shell, all the fire inside him snuffed out. I tagged along with the cop who was officially in charge when he went to speak to him, and it was like talking to a man who was already gone for good.

We got through the routine questions. Farrell responded like a robot. Then the cop said, 'Had you noticed anybody hanging around who shouldn't have been?'

Farrell's eyes lost their dullness and his body tensed. 'If I had, I would have dealt with it,' he snarled.

'What do you mean, "dealt with it"?' I asked.

Farrell's gaze raked me from head to toe. He seemed almost to gather himself together, as if he had just realized Katie's death might not be the only bad thing that could happen tonight. 'I would have called the police,' he said. 'What do you think I meant?'

I said nothing, holding his hot stare with my eyes. At last, I broke the silence. 'What about enemies?' I said. 'Is there anybody who might have a grudge against you? Somebody you might have provoked?' I kept my voice calm and steady, acting as if I didn't have a clue about the sort of life he led.

'Are you trying to say this is my own fault?' The robot was gone and a man in pain had stepped out of the shadows. His face twisted with emotion. 'This isn't normal. This isn't what happens when you piss somebody off. This is some nutter that's done this.' He turned away, pulling the blanket close as if he'd only just noticed how cold it was. 'Leave me in peace to grieve for my Katie,' he said, so quiet I almost didn't catch it.

He walked away. I went to follow him, but the local cop grabbed my arm. 'For Christ's sake,' he said, looking at me like I was less than human. 'The man's just lost his kid.'

I shrugged his hand off. 'You really have no idea who you're dealing with, do you? Let me tell you something about Jack Farrell. If he thought killing somebody's kid was the best way to get their attention, he'd do it without a second thought. The only surprise is that somebody had the balls to do it to him first.'

CHAPTER TWO

FOUR HOURS LATER, WE moved in on the local boys. My boss made it clear to their boss that we would run the game. They weren't happy about it, mostly because they would still be doing all the donkey work while we sat in the shadows and reaped the benefit.

I dished out the tasks at the morning meeting. I sent one team to go and see Farrell's wife Martina, who was holed up in their Chelsea flat. The Spanish nanny had been taken to hospital suffering from smoke inhalation, so I sent another team round to talk to her as soon as she was up to it.

Of course, they didn't have a clue where Jack Farrell had gone to ground. Shortly after I'd spoken to him, a Jeep Cherokee had shown up, driven by a shaven-headed thug I recognized as one of Farrell's top lads. Farrell had climbed aboard and they'd taken off. I assumed the local cops had demanded to know where they were going. But no. They'd let him swan off God knows where with nothing but his lawyer's phone number as security.

I wasn't worried, though. They might not know where Jack Farrell was, but I knew where he'd be. I knew he was a man of regular habits. We'd had a close tail on him a few months back, and his daily routine never altered. It didn't take many days for us to understand how he'd stayed a cleanskin this long. He knew exactly how to stay one step ahead. Keeping tabs on him was pointless. Jack Farrell never put a foot wrong. I've been doing this job for half a dozen years now and I've never come across anybody who took so many pains to make sure he stayed untouchable.

I called over the two detectives from the local squad who looked least stupid. 'I expect you know by now that Jack Farrell's a bad lad. Now, I want you to talk to Farrell again,' I said. 'Nothing too heavy, just go through last night one more time. But press him a bit harder on why anybody would want to target his lovely little girl.'

They swapped uneasy glances. 'We don't know where Farrell is, Mr Martin,' the younger one said, his neck turning pink in embarrassment.

'I know that. And I'm not exactly sure where he is right this minute either. But I think I know where we can pick him up. Here's how it used to go every morning before today. At half past seven, a black BMW four-wheel drive rolls up at the gates of Jack Farrell's mansion. At the wheel, Francis Riley, known as Fancy. He's the number three man in Farrell's squad. In the passenger seat, Danny Chu, Farrell's number two.

'They drive up to the house and out pops Farrell in running shorts and vest. Chu gets out of the 4∞4, also in running gear, and takes a suit carrier from the Spanish nanny, who's lurking in the doorway. He stows the suit carrier in the car, then Chu and Farrell set off across the grounds at a nice steady pace. With me so far?'

The two of them nodded like a pair of puppets.

'Three miles of open country later, the pair of them jog into the car park of Smithson's, which I am told is the most select leisure club in Hampshire. That's where Fancy Riley waits with the suit carrier. The three men go inside together. Chu heads for the steam room while Riley and Farrell swim twenty lengths then spend ten minutes in a very noisy spa pool.

'Then they sit and have breakfast in the club restaurant. Same table every day. Where they talk about sport, their families and the money markets.'

I knew that because we'd had the table bugged. But you can't bug a swimming pool or a spa pool. And whatever they might be able to do on the TV, in real life it's almost impossible to pick up conversation between two men jogging across open country.

A couple of days of shadowing Jack Farrell, and we'd known exactly how his empire ran itself. Chu and Riley reported to Farrell during their morning exercises and Farrell issued his orders at the same time. They never spoke about their illegal businesses in their cars, their offices, their homes or their regular restaurants. Anywhere it was possible to be electronically overheard, Jack Farrell came off like he was Mr Clean. The routine was a strength. But it could also be a weakness.

I smiled at the two rural cops. 'And that's where you're going to find Jack Farrell – in his jogging shorts, in the car park of Smithson's. Failing that, you're just going to have to spoil his poolside breakfast, aren't you?'

They looked a little doubtful. The younger one, a carrot-top with freckles like a bad rash, said, 'His kid's just burned to death. You think he's going to be swimming laps at the health club?' His voice rose in a squeak at the end of the question.

Detective Sergeant Ben Wilson, my bagman on all our major operations, leaned into the chat. 'Well, it's not like he's going to have to worry who's doing the school run, now, is it?'

They both recoiled as if they'd been slapped. I gave Ben a hard stare. The low-level locals always hate us for steaming in on their patch. There's no need to give them more reason for their dislike. 'Ignore him,' I said, trying to sound like we were all comrades together. 'He was brought up by wolves. Yes, I do think he's going to be at the health club, and here's why.

'Whoever did this, they did it so that Jack Farrell would fall. Whether they did it for revenge or to move in on his business, it's all about cutting him off at the knees. I've been watching Farrell for a long time, and I think

11

they've got it wrong. Katie's death isn't going to make Farrell throw in the towel. It's going to make him dig his heels in. Not only is he going to stay on top, he's going to crush anybody he thinks might have had a hand in what happened to his girl. So he's got orders to issue today. And that, boys, is why he's going to be at the health club.' I sent them on their way, positive I was right on the money.

Pride comes before a fall, they say. So I should have been ready for the fact that everything would be tits-up by lunchtime.

CHAPTER THREE

THE FIRST TEAM BACK were the ones I'd sent to talk to Martina in the plush white flat with the high ceilings and the river view. I knew as soon as they walked in it hadn't gone well. Heads down, shoulders hunched, they'd lost all the bounce they'd walked out the door with a few hours before.

They plodded up to the desk I'd taken over. 'Well?' I asked, eyebrows raised.

'No, not well,' the woman DC said. 'She's off her face.'

'She's off the planet,' her partner said. 'On drugs. Not the kind you take when you go out clubbing on a weekend. More the kind that tame doctors feed you when they want to keep you from thinking about your kid being dead.'

'The doctor's got her dosed up to the eyeballs on tranks,' the woman said. 'We're not going to get any sense out of her. Probably not in this lifetime, anyway.'

'You think the doctor's under Farrell's orders?' I asked. I was interested in how it seemed to people who were out of the loop on Farrell's track record.

The woman shrugged. 'You lose a kid like that, you're going to want to be well out of it. I think the doctor's giving her what she wants.'

'Yeah, and when she comes back from her space walk, who knows what she'll remember,' her buddy added gloomily.

I had to agree with him. It didn't look like Martina was going to be much use. In that state, she couldn't tell us anything useful about who might want to burn her daughter to death or why. Even more importantly, from Farrell's point of view, she couldn't tell us where he was or what he was up to.

It got worse when the second team drifted back towards lunchtime. They'd gone out looking keen and sharp, the way young CID lads get when they have something to prove. Now they looked shifty, rather than pissed off like the earlier pair. My heart sank. *That's what you get when you send boys on a man's errand,* I thought to myself. *They've been blown out.*

Turned out, it was worse than that. 'She's

done a runner,' the shorter, skinnier one said; Laurel to the other one's Hardy. Not that there was much to laugh about.

Hardy nodded miserably. 'Not a Scooby-Doo where she is. The hospital treated her for the effects of the smoke, then discharged her. We had a couple of uniforms waiting to talk to her, but she said she was too upset. She said Farrell had told her to check into a local hotel, so our lads dropped her off at the door. But she never checked in.' He looked at his shoes. It seemed like he was as impressed with his co-workers as I was.

'Wonderful,' I said bitterly. 'I don't suppose you checked any other local hotels? Just on the off-chance?'

'That's what took us so long,' the skinny one said. 'Nobody locally has her registered.'

I sighed and shook my head. 'OK. We're probably too late now, but get on to the airports and the airlines. Let's see if Manuela has already skipped off back to Spain. And if she hasn't, put out an alert at all points of exit.' I waved them away and swung round to face Ben Wilson.

'I'm beginning to wonder if I was right about Farrell sticking to his usual routine,' I said.

Ben gave his nicotine gum a vigorous chew, a look of disgust on his bulldog face. 'We'll find out soon enough,' he said, nodding towards the door. 'They're back. And it looks like they're empty-handed.'

I swung round in the direction of his gaze. The two lads I'd sent out to bring me Jack Farrell had just come in. There was an empty space between them where Farrell should have been. 'He never showed, guv,' the ginger one said as soon as he was close enough to tell me without shouting.

'I'm not your guv,' I said sharply. 'Which I regard as a result, frankly. You're telling me Jack Farrell hasn't been near Smithson's today?'

They both nodded.

'What about Danny Chu and Fancy Riley? Did they turn up?' I asked.

The red-haired lad flashed a quick glance at his oppo. A glance that said, *Oh, shit.* They both shifted from one foot to the other.

'Never mind,' I sighed. 'OK, here's what I want you to do. Phone Farrell's lawyer and set up a meeting down here. Tell him we need to take a formal statement from Farrell about the fire. Tell him it needs to be sooner rather than later.'

They slunk off, leaving me with Ben. 'What do you think?' I said.

Ben spat his gum into the bin and shrugged. 'Katie was his only kid. Maybe he really is beside himself with grief.'

I wasn't won over by the argument. Even less so when the fat lad I'd put on Manuela's tail came back to me later on.

'She was on the first flight from Heathrow to Malaga. She was on the ground there three hours ago, but she hasn't shown up at the family home,' he said. 'The Spanish cops checked it out. Her mum and dad only live an hour from the airport. They claim they had no idea she was on her way back to Spain. And they haven't a clue where she might be holed up.'

Like most English gangsters, Farrell had connections in Spain. That's probably how he'd got Manuela in the first place. It's still easy to disappear there. So many tourists, so many short-term workers. I remember once meeting a Spanish cop who said there were some parts of his country where there were no locals any more. Somewhere like that would be the perfect place to stash a young Spanish woman you wanted to stay hidden for a while. For whatever reason.

I looked at Ben. 'Farrell had enough wits about him to get the nanny out of the picture,' I said, grim-faced. 'Still think he's so upset he's lost it?'

CHAPTER FOUR

THE LAWYER GOT BACK to us towards the end of the afternoon. His name was Max Carter and his voice irritated the hell out of me, never mind what he had to say. He made Prince Charles sound common as muck. The upshot was, Jack Farrell was willing to meet us the next morning at the lawyer's office.

'I'd rather Mr Farrell came down to the police station,' I said. 'I'm going to be a bit pushed for time tomorrow morning and I want to take a formal statement.'

'We're all busy men,' Carter said in a lofty way that made me long to slap him. 'However, neither of us has lost a child in the last twenty-four hours. Mr Farrell deserves our compassion and our consideration. A police station is not equipped to provide either of those, Detective Chief Inspector. Shall we say ten thirty at my office?'

I didn't have much choice, so I agreed. As I

put the phone down, I turned to Ben and told him about the meeting. 'Carter's office is in one of those Canary Wharf towers. I want a pair of officers on all the ground-level exits and two cars in the underground car park. See if we can chase up the building plans from the council, just to be on the safe side. Farrell doesn't get out of there without a tail.'

Ben nodded. 'OK, boss. Do you want me to get a tap on the lawyer's phone?'

'He'll assume we've already got one. Besides, there's no point. Every move we make just shows us how canny Farrell is. Even now the arse has dropped out of his world, the firewalls are still holding firm. You might want to tap up some of the usual sources and see if we can track down Danny and Fancy, though.' I shut up sharpish as a tall woman stopped by my desk. Her thick dark hair had a distinctive silver streak falling from the centre parting over one ear. I grinned at the sight of her.

'You're a bit off your patch, aren't you?' I said.

'I could say the same to you,' she replied. She pointed to Ben's chair and he stood up with a twisted little smile. She swung round the desk and settled down, propping her feet on the bin with a sigh of pleasure.

I've always admired a woman who can stand up for herself. Dr Stella Marino had enough bottle to stand up for her entire sex. For the last five years, she'd been cutting up bodies for me. Unlike the ones that Farrell carved up, the ones Stella worked on were already dead.

'I'm not your personal pathologist, you know,' she said now. 'You're not the only bunch of cops who need to call on the best.'

'You're here for Katie Farrell?' I knew the answer, but you have to go through the motions, even when you work as closely together as Stella and I do.

Stella nodded. 'Though only because of your interest in her father, I suspect. There was nothing about the body to suggest anything other than what you all assumed at the time. She was in her bed. The smoke and fumes killed her. The body was badly burned, but that happened post mortem. I suppose that may offer some comfort to her parents.' She tried not to sound bored but failed. Poor Stella gets bored very quickly when a body offers no surprises.

'You're saying the person who did this didn't want her to suffer?' Ben chipped in.

Stella pushed her hair back from her face in a familiar gesture. 'Motive's your thing, Ben. I just read what's written on the body.' She yawned then got to her feet. 'You'll get the formal report in a day or two.'

'Let me walk you out,' I said, falling into step beside her. When we'd got beyond the reach of Ben's flapping ears, I spoke. 'It's been a while, I know, but it looks like I might have some free time this evening. I could bring a takeaway round to yours?'

Stella bit her lip. 'It's a nice thought, Andy. But here's the thing. I'm off to the States at the end of the week and I've got a million things to do before I leave.'

'The States?' I tried not to slide straight into a huff, but it was a struggle. OK, we're not exactly what you'd call an item, Stella and me. But getting together three or four times a month for dinner and a session between the sheets isn't nothing either. 'It's the first I've heard about the States.'

We were out in the hall by now, shoulder to shoulder in the narrow passage. Stella didn't slow down, just kept heading for the lifts with her long stride. 'I got the chance to spend a month at the Body Farm,' she said. 'You know, where they –'

'I know what they do there,' I cut in. 'Hard to resist. A month watching bodies rot. A pathologist's wet dream.' I shook my head and let my mouth curl into a sneer. 'Beats hanging out with me and a Chinese.'

Stella stabbed the lift button and swung round to face me. 'Listen to yourself. I've heard five-year-olds sounding more adult.' Stella laughed and leaned forward to plant a soft kiss on my cheek. She smelled, as she always did at the end of a working day, of the lavender gel she scrubbed her face and hands with. 'Silly boy,' she said. She patted my arm as the lift doors opened. 'I'll see you when I get back. Try not to find any really interesting bodies between now and then.'

I faked a glare. 'I'll see what I can come up with. Just to spite you.'

CHAPTER FIVE

THE STAKE-OUT HAD BEEN in place for a full hour before the meeting at Max Carter's office. Even though we do this sort of thing all the time, I think we were all a bit edgy that morning. The game had changed somehow and it felt like we didn't quite know the new rules yet.

We picked up Farrell as soon as he was dropped off outside the building by Fancy Riley just after ten. The apparent change in him was striking. He walked the short distance to the main door like an old man, his shoulders hunched and his walk hesitant. His head was bowed, his eyes fixed on the pavement. To be honest, I might have walked past him in the street without recognizing him if I hadn't been keeping an eye out for him.

'He looks like shit,' Ben said.

'No wonder.'

'You think it's for real?' he asked.

'You're the one with kids,' I said. 'How would

you be feeling if that was Owen or Bethan on the slab?'

Ben took a moment to think. 'Angry,' he said at last, rubbing a hand over the blond stubble that covered his cannonball head. 'Angry is what I'd be feeling. I'd be raging to get my hands on the person that killed my kid. I'd be storming in there with my fists at the ready. But Farrell just looks beaten. He looks like a man who's thrown in the towel. Only goes to show, you can never tell the thing that will truly cut somebody off at the knees. Before this, I would not have believed Jack Farrell would take this lying down.'

As often happened, Ben had put his finger right on the very thing that was bothering me. Jack Farrell was a man of action. We'd seen it time and time again. Someone would try to inflict some serious damage on part of his empire, and Farrell would swing into action. There would be a morning meeting as per usual. Then Danny Chu and Fancy Riley would spend the rest of the day running round like somebody had lit a bonfire under their arses. Within a matter of days, Farrell would be back on top, often stronger than before. And whoever had been dumb enough to try it on was never going to do that again.

Of course, nobody had ever hit on the idea of doing something this personal before. And yet the very idea of Farrell taking this lying down was something we were both struggling with.

But when we walked into Max Carter's office, it looked like that was just what we were going to get. Farrell barely looked up when we were shown in. He was slumped in an armchair, hair greasy and lank, suit crumpled and his eyes dull as pebbles. It was hard to square this hollow shell with the man who ran one of the toughest criminal empires in the country.

When we introduced ourselves, posing as members of the Hampshire force, Farrell made no sign of knowing me from the night of the fire. Carter kept up a steady flow of plummy nothings as he settled us all round a low coffee table, but he couldn't put off our questions for ever.

I took Farrell through the evening leading up to the fire. 'I wasn't home when Katie went to bed,' he said, his voice slow and dull. 'I was late getting back from a meeting in London. But I looked in on her when I got in.'

'What time was that?' Ben asked.

'About half past nine,' Farrell said. 'Then I went in to give her a kiss on my way to bed. Just like I always did.'

And so on. The alarm had been set. At least, he was ninety-nine per cent sure he'd set it like he always did. He'd taped a football match earlier in the evening so he'd gone to bed around half past ten to watch it there. Martina had joined him some time during the second half, before the Arsenal goal. They'd turned out the light just after midnight and gone to sleep.

The smell of smoke had woken Martina first. She had shaken him awake and he'd jumped out of bed. 'No, I didn't look at the clock,' he said, his voice weary and sad. 'I ran out of the bedroom and I could see smoke in the hall.'

I stopped him there and Ben took out a floor plan of the house. It was laid out like three sides of a square. The middle section contained public rooms the size of hotel ballrooms. The right-hand side held Farrell's office, Martina's private sitting room, and their bedroom. On

27

the left, there was Katie's playroom, her bedroom and Manuela's two rooms. 'Show me where you saw the smoke,' I said.

He pointed to the hallway that led from his bedroom to the living area. He seemed almost listless and bored, as if his mind was somewhere far away. 'I ran towards the smoke. By the time I got halfway across the main hall, the smoke was so thick I couldn't breathe. I couldn't see any flames, the smoke was too heavy. But I could feel the heat.'

Farrell had struggled back to his bedroom, coughing and gagging. Martina had already called the fire brigade. Together, they'd left the building by the garden door at the far end of the hall. Farrell had run across to the other wing, where Katie slept. He'd been yards away when he realized he was too late. Her bedroom window was a wall of flame. He'd been on his knees facing it, tears running down his face, when the firemen had found him.

The firemen had also found Manuela collapsed on the ground next to the chair she'd used to smash her own bedroom window. Like all the other rooms in that wing of the house, her room had been gutted by the fire. She was lucky to be alive, according to the chief fire officer.

'Is that what you think?' I said to Farrell.

For the first time that morning, his eyes showed some of his old spark. 'What do you mean?'

'Do you think she's lucky to be alive? Or do you think she's alive because that's how she planned it?'

He flicked his wrist like a man batting at a fly. 'Don't be stupid,' he said. 'Manuela loved Katie. They were like sisters.'

'But they weren't sisters. And even sisters have their price,' I said. 'Something like this, is always easier if it's an inside job. Could somebody have got to Manuela?'

For a fleeting moment, I could see Farrell consider the odds. Then he shook his head. 'No way,' he said.

I believed him. And I thought I understood the reason for his faith. Getting her out of the country so fast hadn't just been to protect her. It had also been to protect him. He knew Manuela hadn't killed his daughter because he also knew she was in love with him. Whether he loved her in return, I had no way of knowing. But I'd have staked my pension on the fact that he was making the most of Manuela's feelings.

And that Martina knew nothing about the affair.

CHAPTER SIX

OF COURSE, MAX CARTER kicked us out of the office ahead of Farrell. I wouldn't have been surprised if he'd had a discreet tail on us to make sure we left the building. Ben and I crossed the street and bought a couple of over-priced coffees that had longer names than most of the people I knew. Ben checked that all the stake-out teams were in place. We put our earpieces in so we could hear the radio traffic, then we stared glumly at each other.

'Why do I feel like we're on the road to nowhere?' I said.

'Because that's what Farrell wants you to feel?'

I took a sip. My coffee tasted burnt. It made me wonder how those expensive coffee shops ever caught on in the first place. 'Maybe. Or maybe not. I got the initial forensics report this morning. They've got nothing to go on. The petrol could have come from any one of three thousand odd petrol stations. They got in through the garden door at the far end of the hall, bypassed the alarm sensor on the door. Not exactly easy, but not rocket science either. They left no prints, and the wire they used to bypass the alarm could have been bought anywhere. Any other trace of evidence was destroyed by the fire.'

'It's a right bastard, fire,' Ben said.

Before I could agree, voices crackled in my ear. 'He's on the move,' I said, listening hard.

'He's in lift number six,' I heard. 'Kirsty's in with him. Going down.'

A pause, then, 'He hasn't got out on the ground floor. I couldn't see if he's still in the lift.'

DC Kirsty Blythe's voice cut in next. 'We're on the lower car park level. Subject headed left.' Static crackled in my ear. I was on my feet now, swigging back the coffee and heading for the door. We had two unmarked cars in the car park, one on each level. 'Oh shit,' I heard Kirsty say. 'There's three identical white vans parked side by side. Target's walked in behind them. I can't see which van he's got into.'

Now we were running, Ben and me. No clear

plan of action, except that we couldn't just sit there and do nothing. A black cab came towards us and I hailed him, dragging my warrant card out of my pocket and waving it at him as we piled in. 'Swing round so we can see the exit of the car park for that building there,' I shouted.

Muttering something rude, he did as I asked. We had just got into position when the first of three white vans emerged at the top of the ramp. The first one went left, the second and third right. Our unmarked cars were hot on their tails, one swinging in either direction. I told the cabbie to tuck in on the right.

Ben got on his mobile to the tail car we were behind and told him to stay with the lead van and to leave the second one to us. But I knew we were completely screwed. It's not like on the telly where they make it look like a piece of piss to follow a car without being spotted. You can't tail a vehicle without them realizing it unless you've got two or more cars on the job. It's fine on main routes in the city or out on the motorway. But as soon as you start moving through side streets or country roads, it's all over. Your target knows you're there, so they either lead you in the wrong direction or they lose you.

Our van led us north, sticking with main roads all the way. We ended up horsing it up the M11 towards Cambridge. After about an hour of stupidity, the van turned off and drove down country lanes, bringing us at last to the car park of a village pub. The van pulled in while we hung back, trying to pretend there was nothing unusual about a London taxi idling in some Essex hamlet.

The van driver knew, of course. He got out and walked round to the back of the van. He opened the doors then turned and waved to us. 'Smartarse,' Ben growled.

'Go and check, all the same,' I said.

Ben gave me a dirty look but did as he was told. He walked down the lane and into the car park, casting an idle glance at the open van as he strolled towards the pub. He walked inside. A moment later my phone rang. 'Clean as a whistle,' Ben said. 'I'll be back out as soon as I've finished my pint.'

Neither of the other tail cars had done any better. The van that had turned left had headed into Central London then doubled back. They'd

34

lost him when he shot through a set of traffic lights on the Farringdon Road just as they turned to red. He'd nearly been sideswiped by a bus, but he'd made it.

Our boys hadn't.

The third van had ended up going through the Dartford Tunnel and heading round the M25. They'd lost him in the approach to some roadworks, when a lorry had cut in front of our car at the last minute as the lanes merged. By the time our guy could get clear, there was no chance of reconnecting with the right white van.

At the end of the meeting in Max Carter's office, I'd almost been convinced that Farrell's grief was real. But the stunt with the vans was so like the old Jack Farrell that I didn't know what to think.

CHAPTER SEVEN

OVER THE NEXT FEW days, I got more and more wound up about Jack Farrell. It was as if he had gone up in a puff of smoke. We had sources inside his posse, but they swore that they hadn't seen hide nor hair of the top man. Riley and Chu had never been more visible nor more busy, but as far as Farrell was concerned, he might as well have been the invisible man.

Martina had finally surfaced enough to tell us she didn't know where her husband was. She didn't seem to think there was anything strange about her husband going off the map in the wake of her only child's murder. Which just goes to show how true it is that the very rich are very different from the rest of us. All she seemed to care about was when she could hold the funeral.

Of course, we were also nosing around, trying to put a face to the mystery man who had had the balls to take such a terrible step against

Farrell. But we were getting nowhere on that either. Nobody, it seemed, was prepared to admit they were bold or stupid enough to have taken Katie Farrell's life. It was a genuine mystery.

I missed Stella too. OK, sometimes I didn't see her outside work from one week's end to the next. But that was different from knowing she wasn't around at all. Every night when I got home, pissed off and pent up, I poured myself a large brandy and wished she was there to share it. Then I fell into bed and slept like the dead. Given that, maybe it was just as well she was away.

Five days after the murder of Katie Farrell, something shifted. One of my snouts called me. 'I got something for you,' he began. No names, no pack drill, that's how these exchanges go. 'We need a face to face.'

Two hours later, I was sitting in the back row of a cinema out in the sticks watching a very strange Danish/Scottish film about a homeless transvestite. Sometimes this job is just plain madness. Half an hour into the film, a figure slipped into the seat next to mine.

'All right, Mr Martin?'

'I'd be happier if you had better taste in films, Shanky,' I grunted.

'I thought we'd be safe here from any of Jack Farrell's mob,' Shanky said.

All at once I regained the will to live. 'You got something on Farrell?' I said.

'Not *on* Farrell, as such. More *about* Farrell, you might say.'

'Can we get to the point, Shanky? I haven't got time for one of your round-the-houses tales.'

'This is worth something, Mr Martin,' he said. 'More than the usual.'

'Shanky, I'll take care of you. Just give me what you've got.' It's always a bloody to-and-fro with snouts. All they care about is how much kudos or cash they can squeeze out of you. I hate having to deal with them, but it's part and parcel of how the game works.

'He's shedding,' Shanky said.

'What?' For a moment, I had a bizarre image of Jack Farrell as a shaggy dog, leaving his hairs on the chairs.

'He's off-loading. He's selling off the business in chunks. All for cash. The girls have already gone to some Lithuanian godfather. Danny

Chu's selling his soul to raise enough cash to take over the drugs, and Fancy Riley's got his name down for the loan-sharking. All the other stuff – it's up for grabs. He's talking to people he's been at daggers drawn with for years. People who've tried to take it off him and failed. He's sitting down with slags he wouldn't normally be seen dead with.'

I could hardly believe it. 'What's his game?'

Shanky cleared his throat, a wet, sloppy sound. 'They're saying it's his kid. That he's lost it.'

'And has he?'

Shanky shifted in his seat. 'Jack Farrell? I don't think so. He's still not taking any crap from anybody. He might be selling up, but he's not giving it away. I think he's just had enough. He wants to cash in his chips and fuck off to the sun.'

'Where's he living?' I asked.

'No fucking idea,' Shanky said. 'He's got a boat down Southampton, that's where he's doing the meetings. But he's not living there. What I hear, Fancy takes him off at the end of the day in a big fuck-off speedboat and they're off down the estuary.'

I asked some more, but Shanky had given me all he knew. I handed over an envelope of cash, promising him another wedge if he could come up with any more info.

Back at the office, Ben and I chewed over Shanky's info. It didn't make sense to me. If he was so upset by Katie's death, how could he be arsed to jump through all the hoops involved in taking apart something on this scale? But if he wasn't upset by Katie's death, why bother doing it at all?

'Maybe he needs the money,' Ben said.

'You don't think he's got enough salted away in his various accounts?'

'Can you ever have enough?'

I shrugged. 'I don't know. But I'll tell you what I do wish I knew. I wish I knew what the hell he's planning on doing with all that money.'

CHAPTER EIGHT

IF I'D MADE A LIST of possible reasons why Jack Farrell was turning his business empire into cash, I would never have come up with the truth. But a couple of days later, it seemed as if my question had been answered in a very strange way.

I was sitting in my office, working through what little material we'd gathered on Farrell's bargain basement sale. I was glad to be back in my own office, glad to shake the country bumpkin dust of Hampshire off my shoes. Then Ben walked in, a sheet of paper in his hand.

'What do you know about John Stonehouse?' he said.

'Labour Cabinet minister in the Sixties, fiddled a load of money he couldn't pay back,' I said, dredging my memory. 'Faked a suicide by leaving his clothes on a beach in America with a suicide note. Turned up with his mistress in Australia, where the cops picked him up because they thought he was Lord Lucan. Got extradited, did time. What is this? You doing the *Daily Mail* quick quiz again?'

'Ha ha,' Ben said, dropping the paper on my desk in front of me. 'Just in from our friends in Hampshire.'

I read the memo and whistled. 'And they believe this?'

'His tailor says it's his suit, his cobbler says he made the shoes for him, and Max Carter says he did indeed witness the signature, though he didn't know what the note said.'

'Do you believe it?' I asked.

Ben threw himself into the chair opposite mine. 'No. You don't raise a king's ransom in cash then top yourself. It doesn't make sense.'

'It does if you want to provide for your widow. Martina couldn't run Farrell's business. Even if he was shagging the Spanish nanny, there was still something there with the wife. They still shared a bed, Ben. The only way to make sure she was all right was to make a dash for cash and then stash it somewhere we wouldn't find it.'

Ben looked at me, his mouth open and his eyes wide. 'I can't believe I'm hearing this. You think

Jack Farrell topped himself? You really think the king of smoke and mirrors did himself in?'

I shook my head. 'Not for a minute. But I can see how you could make an argument for it. The guy was destroyed by his kid's death. He couldn't go on. But he cared enough for the mother of his child to make sure she would be OK. It's a strong case and if we're going to knock it down, we need facts. And we haven't got anything on our side of the argument except the fact that we don't appear to have a body. What do we know about the tides and currents where he went in?'

Ben rolled his eyes and got to his feet. 'I'm on it.'

Within the hour, we knew three things about the part of the English Channel where Jack Farrell's clothes had been found. One was that quite a few people choose that part of the coast as their jumping-off point for suicide. Two was that bodies usually took a week to ten days to make their way to shore about fifteen miles west of where they'd gone in. And three was that the combination of marine life and shipping meant the bodies tended to be pretty well mashed up.

While the official line might be that Jack Farrell had topped himself, in private we knew we had to wait and see.

As it turned out, we didn't have to wait very long. Eight days later, we got the call from Dorset police. A body had washed up on a beach near Poole and they had reason to believe (as some cops still feel the need to say) that we might be interested in taking a look at it. Why might that be, we asked. On account of the tattoos, they said, a bit stiff.

Ben didn't hang about. It was pedal to the metal with our blue light flashing all the way down there. I missed Stella every mile of the way. Sure, she wasn't the only competent pathologist in the world. But we made a good team. She understood what we needed, she was fast and she was damn good in the witness box.

Usually a body that's been in the sea a couple of weeks is hard to identify. The face and head get bashed about against rocks. Fingerprints get nibbled by crabs. Bodies change shape in the water. They get bloated and stop looking like themselves. That's when you need a pathologist to read the body and tell you what you're looking at. And to take the samples so you can check DNA.

We knew from the Dorset cops that this corpse's head and hands were in bad shape. But as soon as we walked into the mortuary, I knew we weren't going to need Stella to identify this particular corpse. The colours were faded, the shapes contorted because the skin was stretched and torn. But the tattoos were unmistakable.

The dragon I'd seen on the night of the fire still covered his torso, its tail snaking down his naked groin to taper to an end on his left thigh. The flame of its breath was dulled now, but we could still see it clearly crossing the right side of his chest, climbing up to his shoulder. One arm was torn off halfway down, but the top half of the samurai remained. On the other arm, the woman looked like she'd gained weight and needed an appointment with the hairdresser.

I reckoned we didn't need to bother Martina. I could ID Jack Farrell on the spot. It looked like I'd been wrong again.

All the same, I did ask the pathologist to take samples for DNA testing. I wanted to compare it with Katie's DNA and with the DNA we'd got from the clothes and the note left on the beach.

Like they say, it's best to use a long spoon when you sup with the devil.

CHAPTER NINE

NOT EVERYBODY THOUGHT I was doing the right thing about the DNA. I'd barely walked through the door the next morning when my boss was on my case. 'What's the point?' he said, face red as a baboon's backside. 'We know it's Farrell. Right age, height, build. The tattoos, for Christ's sake. If ever there was an open-and-shut case, this is it. Andy, it was you that ID'd him. But that's not good enough for you, is it? No, now you want DNA tests. Do you have any idea how much it costs to even try to get DNA from a badly burned body?'

I shrugged. 'It's Jack Farrell. Better safe than sorry.'

He ran his hand across his stubble scalp. 'They tell me they have to use something called SNIPS. It costs an arm and a leg, and most times it doesn't even bloody work. And in this case it won't prove anything either way. So what if the DNA doesn't match? It doesn't mean that body isn't Jack Farrell. All it means is that Martina Farrell was putting it about a bit.' He threw his hands in the air. 'It doesn't even prove that. For all we know, they could have had fertility treatment. The only DNA comparison worth a toss is with the clothes on the beach. And the letter.'

He had a point, but I wasn't about to admit it. 'So, what? You want me to cancel the tests?'

'No. I already did that, Andy.' He pointed his finger at me. 'You have got to stop running the show like it's your personal bloody empire. I carry the can for you when things go tits-up. The least you can do is run stuff past me.' He sighed. 'I know it's boring, but we've got budgets, Andy.'

'You're right,' I said. He looked shocked, then pleased. But I couldn't help myself. I had to burst his balloon. 'It is boring.' God, I missed Stella. She'd have done the tests and worried about the budget afterwards.

All day, people were dropping in to congratulate us. Like we'd had something to do with Jack Farrell not being our problem any more. Like it was a result. Nobody seemed to want to think about the fact that even if Farrell was dead, his rackets were all still alive and well. Alive and well and being run by people with half his brains and a tiny fraction of his street smarts.

To my mind, that spelled trouble. Farrell's empire had worked because the emperor ran it with a rod of iron. I once read that Nero had said something like, 'Let them hate as long as they fear,' and that was how Jack Farrell did business. I didn't think either Danny Chu or Fancy Riley could hold a candle to their dear departed boss in the fear stakes. Things were going to start falling apart very soon. And then it was all going to be very messy on our patch.

Ben got it, though. 'They'll be fighting over the spoils like dogs with a bag of bones,' he said. 'The fall-out's going to be something else.'

The first victim hit the ground two days after Farrell's body was found. Joey Scardino's family had come to Scotland at the end of the 19th century and had made their living from fish and chips and ice cream. But Joey had seen too many films about the Mob and he'd come to London in search of a more edgy living than fast food. He liked people to call him Joey Scar, and a few sucked up to him enough to do it. I wasn't one of them. I never dignify those scumbags by using their nicknames.

Anyway, Joey was just about clever and charming enough to pass as a gangster, but he'd never managed to be in the right place at the right time. He was desperate to be playing by big boys' rules.

As part of his bid, he'd been snapping at Farrell's heels for a long time. He'd seen how much money Farrell was making from people-smuggling and supplying illegal immigrants with false papers. Scardino wanted to carve out a chunk of the action for himself. But every time he'd tried to muscle in on it, Farrell had found a way to slap him down.

According to Ben, who had been running a low-level snout inside Farrell's posse, Scardino had paid a load of cash to Farrell after the fire. The word was that the money was payment for the business he'd failed to steal in the past. The only trouble was that Scardino wanted a fast return on what he'd laid out. Unlike Farrell, he didn't understand that making a modest amount every week for years was smarter than

CHAPTER TEN

THE ONLY ODD THING about Joey Scardino's death – apart from it being totally disgusting – was that nobody was laying claim to it. The usual routine in murders like this is that the word creeps out. That's how the Jack Farrells of this world create the fear that lets them exercise power. First the villains get to know. Then it filters down to us through our snouts and our undercover cops. There might not be any proof, but everybody who needs to know gets to know.

But with Scardino there wasn't so much as a whisper. The usual suspects were giving each other the hard stare, wondering who had ordered the hit on Scardino. There wasn't even an obvious motive. Yes, Joey Scardino had bought a slice of Jack Farrell's action. And yes, his death meant that slice should end up on somebody else's plate. Most likely the plate of the person who had seen him off. But that wasn't what had happened. Oh no, nothing that simple.

What had happened was that the business had fallen to pieces faster than Patsy Cline. It had split into splinters and now bits of Jack Farrell's fake ID business were being operated by half a dozen slimeballs who had been quick off the mark. There was no single winner from Scardino's death. It really didn't look like he had been topped for the sake of stealing his crummy little racket.

And if not for that, then why?

The second body came five days after Joey Scardino. Brian Cooper and Jack Farrell had both started their lives of crime working for the same boss, a tough old East End gangster called Billy Boardman. They'd both started at the bottom of the totem pole with low-level drug running. But they'd both been too smart to stay at the bottom for long.

Jack had clawed his way up the organization, making it impossible for Billy to do without him. Then Billy had been killed in his bed, a single bullet to the head. What was worse was that his young bride had died alongside him, shot in the same way. Nobody could work out how the assassin got past the security. Well, nobody who didn't know that Jack Farrell had been giving one to the lovely bride.

Farrell got the respect, and most of Billy Boardman's business. But he didn't want Brian Cooper working for him. He knew Cooper was as greedy as he was. He knew Cooper would already be plotting how to get Farrell out of the way. So Farrell and Cooper made a deal.

Cooper would get fencing and faking, and Farrell would get the rest. And they'd stay off each other's turf. Farrell wouldn't send out teams to sell fake Rolexes, and Cooper wouldn't run drugs or prostitutes. It was a split that had worked well for a long time. But in the past few months, some cracks had started to appear in the deal.

It was Farrell who had started being a bit naughty, by all accounts. He was bringing more and more girls in from the former Eastern Bloc countries, where a lot of the brand-name fakes came from. And instead of abiding by the old borders and selling them on to Cooper, Farrell had started a team of youths flogging the fakes round the pubs and the markets.

Cooper had been well pissed off. He'd even gone so far as to turn up at Farrell's office in Soho to sound off about it. Farrell had been livid. The Soho office was for his above-board business. Nothing criminal crossed the threshold there. Least of all a gangster like Cooper who had failed to rub off his East End rough edges.

Cooper had demanded 'tax' on Farrell's new scam with the fakes. The version I heard was that Farrell had laughed in his face. Farrell told Cooper the only reason Cooper still had a business at all was that he, Farrell, had a soft spot for him because of the old days. Then Farrell told Cooper that in future he, Cooper, would be paying 'tax' to Farrell as the price of being allowed to stay in business at all.

Cooper had stormed off, mouthing all sorts of threats against Farrell. The row had blown up a couple of weeks before the fire, and Cooper had been one of the evil bastards we'd taken a good look at. Of course, he had an alibi. Men like Brian Cooper always do because they are seldom the ones who do the dirty work with their own hands. But it wasn't a very solid alibi. It sounded too genuine. It didn't feel like one he'd had in place because he knew he'd need it. And that made me think he wasn't expecting Katie to die that night. That in turn meant he probably hadn't ordered the hit. Still, he had been on my list.

But Cooper clearly had more people on his case than Jack Farrell. And one of them had got rid of him in a very ugly way.

CHAPTER ELEVEN

BRIAN COOPER HAD TAKEN a long time to die. And it hadn't been a good time. He'd been murdered in the warehouse where he stored his stock. His killer had tied him to a chair then put his feet in buckets of fast-setting concrete. Once he was sure Cooper wasn't going anywhere, the murderer had cut into his veins at the wrists and the elbows. Cooper had bled out, naked, trapped and most likely alone.

I stood in the warehouse, trying not to look at the bloody mess. But it drew my eyes back time and time again, as if it was a magnet and I was the iron filings. First Joey Scardino and now Brian Cooper. Somebody out there was trying to carve out an empire for himself and he was doing it in the most brutal and heartless way he could think of.

If I had been a criminal near the top of the tree, I'd have been gibbering with fear. I'd have locked myself into my most secure room, armed to the teeth with guns and bullets, and stayed there till the war to fill Jack Farrell's shoes was over.

I'd still have had to come out one day and face the last man standing. But at least the odds would be in my favour. I'd know where to look.

Of course, I was on the other side of the law. I was the one charged with finding out who was behind this before there was only one man left standing. If I left it till then, I'd be too late. Everybody would be locked into the new regime. They'd be too afraid to turn in the brute who had the power of life and death over all of them. The king is dead. Long live the king.

It was cold in the warehouse and I shivered, in spite of my warm coat. I turned to my sergeant. 'Any ideas, Ben?'

He gave a weary sigh. 'None that make any sense. We've got plenty of bad lads to choose from, but I can't think of anybody as extreme as this.'

I knew what he meant. Violence like this doesn't just spring up from nowhere. It has roots. It takes time to develop. And I couldn't put a name to the person who had reached this level of sadistic bloodshed. 'It's got to be a new face,' I said.

'Russians? Chechens?' Ben asked.

'Could be.' I sighed. 'Why can't they just stick to football?'

'Not enough money in it, boss. Not unless you're David Beckham.' Ben sneaked a look at what remained of Brian Cooper. 'Whoever he is, he's sending a message loud and clear.'

'Yeah. "Farrell's gone and I'm the new king of the world,"' I said. 'We need to put some pressure on our snouts. They seem to have gone very quiet all of a sudden.' I roused myself, rolling my shoulders and stamping my feet on the cold cement. 'Time to rattle a few cages, I think.'

'Leave it with me, boss. I'll put the word out,' Ben said.

I nodded. It was good to have someone to rely on for the legwork. Ben had been the one person I'd been adamant about bringing with me when I made the move to Serious Crimes. We knew our way round each other and I knew I could trust him to do what needed to be done. It also didn't hurt that he looked like the hardest bastard on legs. You had to see him with his kids to understand what a pose that was.

'We any further forward on who killed Katie Farrell?' I asked as we walked back to the car.

Ben shook his head. 'Not a whisper.'

'I'd have thought with Farrell out of the way there would be no shortage of takers,' I said. 'Who could resist the chance to look so bold when there's no chance of payback?'

Ben spat a wad of nicotine gum on the ground as we came out of the warehouse into the cold raw air of the morning. 'Good point. But I reckon whoever did it knows there's no mileage in claiming it. Killing Jack Farrell would have been something to shout about. But burning a nine-year-old to death? I don't think there's many would be too quick off the mark to claim that.'

'Maybe so. But I still don't like the fact that we've not had so much as a whisper.' We headed for our car, walking faster as the wind cut into us.

'When's Stella back?' Ben asked as he tucked himself behind the wheel.

'A week or so.'

Ben gave a little snort of laughter.

'What?' I said. 'You think I'm counting the days or something?'

'I never said a thing, boss,' he replied, starting the engine and reversing out of our parking spot. 'I was just thinking how pissed off she's going to be at missing all these good bodies. First we got Farrell, then we got Joey Scar, and now we've got Cooper. Not that there's any mystery about any of them. But she likes something a bit out of the ordinary, does Stella.'

With anyone else, there might have been suggestive overtones in that last sentence. But Ben knew better than to try to be a smartarse about Stella in front of me. I was sure the two of us were the butt of squadroom jokes. Knowing cops, how could we not be? Still, as long as they kept their seedy little routines behind my back, I didn't much care. The day they dared to try it to my face would be the day I knew I'd lost it. But I planned to make sure that day stayed a long way down the road.

'Well, she can always pull out the drawers down the morgue and take a look at them when she gets back,' I said. 'It's not like they're going anywhere.'

Ben laughed. 'Best place for them. It's a

pity we can't put more of the bastards in a mortuary drawer. It would make our job a lot easier.'

I remembered his words when the next body turned up. He couldn't have been more wrong, as it turned out.

CHAPTER TWELVE

I WAS AT HEATHROW AIRPORT, waiting for Stella to emerge from customs and immigration, when I got the call. The clerk on the other end of the phone didn't have much info. All she could say was that a body had been found in Paddington Basin and that she had been told to let me know about it.

'Do they want me at the scene?' I asked.

'Yes. Soon as you can get there, my screen says.'

'I'll be there,' I said, ending the call. I'd come all the way out here to get Stella and I wasn't going back empty-handed. She wouldn't be much longer, and if she felt up to it, she could always come to the scene with me. It was on the way back to her house in St John's Wood, after all.

I hadn't told Stella I would meet her. I'd got the flight details from her secretary, not from her. I wanted it to be a surprise. So there was no way I was going to walk away right then, not just for a dead body that wasn't going anywhere.

Within a couple of minutes of the phone alert, I saw Stella walking down the concourse towards me. It was a rare treat for me to be able to watch her without her knowing, and I took pleasure in letting my eyes follow the easy swing of her walk. Her hair was pulled back in a pony tail and she looked a bit bleary-eyed, but given that she'd just got off a night flight, she seemed pretty alert. I couldn't help myself. I was grinning from ear to ear.

She was only a few yards away when she spotted me. Her eyebrows shot up in surprise, but the smile followed so fast I knew it was real. I stepped forward and we kissed like friends, cheek to cheek. 'Wow, Andy,' she said, putting down her suitcase and hugging me. 'My very own police escort.'

I let my arms slip around her, smelling lavender and feeling the warmth of her flesh. '"Working together for a safer London,"' I said. 'That's our motto.'

I grabbed the handle of her wheelie suitcase and fell into step beside her. 'Flight OK?' I asked.

'It's over. That's the best thing you can say about any flight,' she said. 'So, how have you been managing without me?'

'Andy the man, or Andy the cop?'

She tucked her arm through mine. 'We're in a public place, Andy. Better stick to the cop angle for now.'

As we made our way to the car, I filled her in on what she'd missed while she'd been watching bodies rotting in the States. By the time I'd finished, we were on the motorway back to London. 'Interesting,' she said. 'Jack Farrell kills himself and the genie is let out of the bottle.'

'Some genie,' I snorted. 'If I had three wishes, I wouldn't spend them like that.'

'You sure? It gets a lot of garbage off the streets.'

She had a point. 'I don't mind losing any of them, it's true. But I could do without the extreme crime scenes.'

'Deep down, Andy, you're a wuss,' Stella said.

We both laughed. Then I said, 'If you really feel like you've been missing out, we could take in a nice fresh corpse on the way back to yours.'

Stella turned in her seat to look at me. 'You know the way to a girl's heart, don't you?'

I risked a quick glance at her. 'I hope so. At least where you're concerned. I missed you, Stella.'

She nodded, as if she got it. 'Nice of you to say so.' She shifted in her seat and put her hand on my thigh. It didn't feel sexual. It just felt like she wanted to be touching me. 'Being apart's useful, though. It made me wonder if it was time for us to rethink what's going on between us.'

This wasn't how I'd planned it out in my head. I thought things would settle right back into the same groove as before. I'd had a month of sleeping on my own and I'd been looking forward to changing that. Time for a bit of sweet talking, I thought. 'Seems like you had to go all the way to America before we noticed how much we care about each other,' I said, patting her hand.

'I wouldn't put it quite like that,' she said slowly. 'I guess what I'm trying to say is that we need to make our minds up.'

I didn't much like the sound of this. 'About what?'

'About being together.' She moved her hand

back into her lap. 'Andy, I'm at a crossroads in my life. At the Body Farm, they made it clear that there was a job for me if I wanted it. Now, I love what I do here. But I know I would also love working there. I can't choose between here and there based only on the job.' She sighed. 'I'd hoped I could work up to this in a more relaxed setting.'

I knew just what she meant. This wasn't the scene I'd imagined on my way to the airport. 'What are you saying, Stella?'

'It's pretty simple, Andy. If I'm going to stay, there needs to be a strong reason why. You could be that reason. But if you're going to be the reason, I need more from you than you were giving me before I went away. I want something more than a friendly fuck.'

I pursed my lips and blew out the breath I'd been holding. It wasn't as bad as I'd feared. 'Stella, I don't know how to …'

'No. Not now,' she said, her tone abrupt. 'Think about it before you say anything. We don't have to rush it.' She sat up straight in her seat, making it clear the subject was closed for the time being. 'Now, didn't you say something about a body?'

CHAPTER THIRTEEN

I WAS STILL REELING FROM Stella's words as I parked beside the other police motors that marked the fringe of the crime scene. But within minutes, they felt totally trivial.

The police tapes marked out an area by one of the giant pillars that held up the raised section of the Westway. It was a classic scrap of urban desert. Scrubby grass, rubbish all around, the stink of engine fumes and decay in the air. Stella grabbed her kitbag from the boot and we walked over to the cluster of white suits that marked the target of our interest.

We were still a few yards away when one man peeled off from the main group and blocked our way. I had a vague memory of meeting him on some training course, but I couldn't recall his name or rank. Luckily, I didn't have to. 'DCI Martin,' he said, voice raised to be heard above the traffic noise. He extended a hand. I was a bit taken aback. Cops don't usually do the handshake thing. As we shook, he carried on. 'John Burton, DI Burton. I'm really sorry about this.'

I shrugged. 'I get called out to stuff all the time. Sometimes it's linked to my beat, sometimes not. Nothing to be sorry about.'

Burton looked confused. 'Did nobody brief you?'

'All I got was a request to attend,' I said. 'Why? Is there something more?'

Burton's eyes were all over the place. He couldn't settle on me or Stella or on anything else. 'Christ,' he said softly. He took my arm and tried to steer me off to one side.

I shook free. 'You can say anything you have to say in front of Dr Marino,' I said. 'If this body's one of mine, she'll be doing the post mortem.'

Burton licked his lips. 'I really am sorry about this,' he said again.

'Can we cut to the chase?' Stella said. 'I've just flown in from America and I need to check this out before I die from lack of sleep.'

Burton nodded and cleared his throat. 'We know who the victim is,' he said, still not meeting my eyes.

I didn't have any sense of looming disaster. None at all. So much for cop instinct. 'Yeah?' I said, edgy at being kept waiting.

Burton took a deep breath. 'It's your bagman. DS Wilson.'

It was like a punch to the throat. I couldn't breathe and my legs felt like I'd run a half marathon. I felt Stella's hand on my arm. That was all that was keeping me steady. 'Ben?' I said, not wanting to believe him.

'No room for doubt. He's got ID on him, and one of my lads trained with him.'

I felt ill. I wanted to collapse to the ground and wrap my arms round my knees. But my feelings would have to wait. I owed it to Ben to find out what had gone down in this hellhole. 'I need to take a look,' I said, moving past Burton.

'I don't think that's a great idea,' he said.

'My bagman, my case,' I said roughly. 'He's mine now.' I strode off to where I knew the body would be, at the centre of the group of white-clad figures. I could sense Stella at my back.

When I saw what was left of Ben, I understood why Burton had wanted me to keep away.

Even Stella, who has seen most of the worst that human beings can do to each other, gasped at the sight.

He was sitting, propped up against one of the pillars. His legs were spread apart, to stop him toppling over. His head lolled to one side, looking quite normal apart from having no face. It had been skinned, like a scalping in reverse. Hair intact, face gone. His torso was naked and he'd been cut from his throat to his navel. He'd obviously been alive when it happened. His hands gripped his internal organs, as if he was trying to push them back inside.

I've never cried at a crime scene before, though God knows I've seen my share of horrors. But I cried for Ben, big fat tears that spilled down my cheeks. I didn't even brush them away. I felt no shame for showing my feelings.

At last, I turned away. Stella was at my shoulder, her face a rigid mask. 'On you go,' I said. 'Find me something to nail this bastard.'

'If it's there, I'll find it,' she said.

Burton was right beside her. 'How do you want to run this?' he said.

'Everything goes across my desk. Get your boss to talk to my boss. We need to be in the loop on this one. We have info you don't, but we'll share on a need-to-know basis. Bottom line is we nail the animal who did this. And I don't give a toss what it takes. The rule book's out of the window on this one.'

Burton nodded. 'I can't fault you on that. I'll make sure we keep you up to speed.'

I took a couple of steps towards my car, then stopped. 'Who found him?' I asked.

'The Fire Brigade.'

'The Fire Brigade? What's that all about?' I was puzzled.

Burton pointed to an area of scorched grass about twenty feet from Ben's body. I hadn't even noticed it. That's how far I was from being a cop right then. 'Someone had lit a fire,' he said. 'Like a beacon or something. A train cleaner going home from Paddington spotted the blaze and called it in. When the firemen got here, they found Sergeant Wilson.' Burton looked away. 'They reckon he wasn't long dead.'

I tried not to think about that. I drove back to my office, wondering about the fire. What was the point of making sure Ben was found quickly? Why shout murder from the rooftops? Mostly, killers want bodies to stay hidden so they have more time to cover their tracks.

Whoever had killed Ben wanted us to know about it. He was sending us a message and he wanted us to get it. Fast.

CHAPTER FOURTEEN

THEY SAY IF A CASE doesn't start to break in the first twenty-four hours, it won't break at all. I've never worked to that belief. If I did, I wouldn't have cleared half the cases I have. If you keep pushing, nine times out of ten something will give. But after five days of getting nowhere, I was starting to fear that Ben's murder might be the one in ten that doesn't crack wide open.

It wasn't for the want of hard work. I knew that every officer on my team was working way over their set hours, not caring whether they were being paid overtime or not. And from what John Burton said, the same was true of his squad. When a cop goes down, that's how it is. Joey Scardino and Brian Cooper were not just on the back burner – they were right outside the kitchen.

I'd hardly seen Stella since the morning of her return. I was working from breakfast to bedtime and beyond, only going home to grab a few hours' sleep when my body and brain could go no further. Stella had done the post mortem report on Ben. Her report had been the most detailed I'd ever seen. But apart from that, I had no idea where she was or what she was doing. So much for working out how we could change things between us. That was going to have to wait until I had put Ben's killer behind bars.

Six days after we'd started the hunt for the monster who had butchered Ben, Stella turned up in my office, looking grave. 'I need to talk to you, Andy,' she said, dropping into the chair opposite my desk. She looked as if she hadn't had much more sleep than I had since her return.

'I'm always glad to hear from you, Stella.' I wasn't flirting and she knew it.

'I've spent most of the last few days out on a limb,' she said. 'I know I should trust the people I work with to do the job properly, but I can't help myself. Call me a control freak, but unless I've done the post mortem myself, I always think there's more to be found.' She looked a bit embarrassed, but I didn't see why she should be. I'm the same myself.

'You're probably right,' I said. 'You being the best, and all.'

She gave me a little look, like she wasn't sure if I was taking the piss. Then she smiled and shrugged. 'Whatever. Anyway, once I'd done all I could with Ben's body, I thought I would take a look at all the other bodies you've been tripping over while I was gone.' She flipped open one of the files she'd brought with her, then looked up at me with earnest eyes. I felt a little stab of dread.

'I want to be clear about this, Andy,' she said. 'Are you tying Ben's death into the other recent murders, or are you treating it as something apart from them?'

I frowned. 'Why would it be connected to Joey Scardino and Brian Cooper? They were killed because somebody's trying to stake a claim to Jack Farrell's empire.'

'I don't know why,' Stella said in that gentle voice she always uses when she thinks I need to be calmed down. 'Maybe Ben got too close to finding out who the new king of the hill is, and had to be silenced.'

I shook my head. 'Not without telling me what he'd found. We were a team, me and Ben.

He wouldn't have kept something that big to himself. But why are you asking me this, Stella? What's your point?'

Stella took out a sheaf of photographs and spread them over my desk. 'The same knife killed Brian Cooper and Ben, Andy.' She tapped the photos, showing me where the cuts and tears matched each other. 'There, and there, and there. The same. It's an unusual knife, that's why there's very little doubt. I think it's one of those fancy cheese knives. You know the ones I mean? They've got a very thin, curved blade with sections cut out of it to make it go through hard cheeses more easily. They've got twin points.'

She pointed to a couple of details. 'You see? Stab marks side by side. I think the killer used one of those cheese knives on Cooper and on Ben.'

It was a struggle to get my head round what Stella was saying. 'That's insane. I can't think of any reason why the person who killed Brian Cooper would have any motive to kill Ben.'

Stella looked uneasy. 'Can we come back to that, please, Andy? I've got something else to tell you. Something that might help to make sense of this.'

'OK,' I said. 'I'm up for anything that stops me feeling like I'm on the wrong side of the looking glass.'

'I thought that I would go back and take another look at Jack Farrell's body.'

'You thinking someone murdered him and made it look like suicide?' I asked. 'That won't fly, Stella. The suicide note was witnessed by his lawyer. He didn't read the contents, but he witnessed the signature.'

Stella's smile was wry. 'That wasn't what I was going to say, Andy.'

'Sorry.' I pulled a face. 'Shouldn't put words in your mouth. Go on. Tell me why you wanted to take a crack at Jack.'

'No reason you could put your finger on. Just that it all started with him. And it's as well I did, really.' She opened the second file she was carrying. From where I was sitting, I could see bar charts and coloured photos of some part of the human body in cross section.

'I checked this three times, just to make sure I was right,' she said, looking me straight in the eye. 'Andy, whoever you've got in that mortuary drawer, it's not Jack Farrell.'

CHAPTER FIFTEEN

I WAS LOST FOR WORDS. 'What do you mean, not Jack Farrell?' I said. 'I made the ID myself.'

'I know, I saw the paperwork. Can I ask you why you ended up doing it?'

'The wife was tranked up to the max, there was no way we could have got her to do it. And I knew it was him.'

'How did you know?' Stella was giving me that wary look, the one she does when she thinks I'm not going to like where she's taking me.

'Because of the tattoos,' I said.

Stella looked grim. 'I thought so. But you were wrong, Andy.'

'Oh, come on, Stella,' I protested. 'You're not telling me there are two blokes walking around with matching tattoos like that. No way.'

'I know it's hard to believe, but if you saw his tattoos while Jack Farrell was alive and well, then this is not his body.'

I shook my head. 'How can you say that?'

'Here's the thing about tattoos. When you have them done, the dye seeps under the skin and into your body's defence system. It's drawn up into the nearest lymph gland, and it stays there, preserved for the rest of your life. If I cut through the lymph glands after you're dead, I can see staining that tells me which part of the body had the tattoo, and what colours it was. In fact, if the tattoo's old, the colours in the lymph gland will probably be brighter than the colours on the skin.'

My mouth had fallen open. 'You're kidding,' I said, remembering to shut it after I'd spoken.

'Deadly serious,' Stella said. 'The first time I came across it was with a torso that washed up on the mud at the Isle of Dogs. I was able to tell you guys that the corpse had had a red and blue tattoo on his left arm and a blue and green one on his right arm. That was enough to ID him from the list of missing persons.'

'OK, OK. But I still don't understand how that tells you this isn't Jack Farrell,' I said.

'This body has clean lymph glands,' Stella said, pointing to some of the cross-section shots.

'I don't get it.'

'The ink only gets drawn up into the lymph glands if you still have a pulse. These tattoos were done after this man died. Not before.' Stella leaned forward, an intense look in her eyes. 'This body cannot be Jack Farrell's.'

I closed my eyes. This felt like a very bad dream. I took a deep breath and glared at Stella. It wasn't her fault, but she was where my face was pointing. 'If you're right, then that means Jack Farrell killed this guy –'

'Or had him killed,' Stella chipped in.

'Or had him killed. Then he had the body tattooed in an exact copy of his own body art, then smashed the face up and made the fingers look like the crabs had been at them.' I ran a hand over my face. The tired sag of my skin matched my feelings pretty closely. 'Those are very extreme steps to make us think he's dead.'

'From everything you've told me about Jack Farrell, extreme is second nature to him,' Stella said.

'But why? What's the point?' I was speaking out loud, but I was talking to myself.

'Maybe his daughter's death scared him?

Maybe he thought he'd be next? Or maybe he'd just had enough of the life,' Stella said.

'Or maybe he wanted a free run at revenge,' I said. 'If Farrell was dead, Katie's killer would be able to relax. And that would make him a lot easier to kill.' I dropped my head into my hands. 'Christ, this turns everything on its head.' Then something struck me. It wasn't a pleasant thought. My stomach churned and I looked up. 'You said something about this helping to make sense of the other cases. Of Ben's murder. What did you mean by that?' I had a shrewd idea, but I wanted to hear it from Stella's lips.

She shook her head. 'You're there already, Andy. Don't make me spell it out for you. I don't want you to blame me for being the one to put the idea into words.' She picked up her files and stood up. 'I'm sorry, Andy. Truly sorry.'

'Wait,' I said. 'Please, sit down.' I swallowed hard. I don't find it easy to ask favours, not even from someone as close as Stella, and I probably sounded gruff.

Stella started to shake her head, then stopped. I guess she saw in my face that I needed something from her. She sat back down. 'What is it?' she said.

'If Jack Farrell is still alive, then we know who killed Joey Scardino and Brian Cooper.' I spoke slowly, as if creeping up on it would somehow make it less painful.

'And we know why,' Stella said.

I nodded. 'Jack thought they had either killed Katie themselves or else they knew who did.' I stretched out a hand and, without having to ask, Stella gave me the first file. I flipped it open. 'And logic suggests that if the same knife killed Brian Cooper and Ben, the same person was using the knife.'

Stella nodded. 'That would seem to make sense.'

'Which means that Jack Farrell killed Ben,' I said, my voice flat and dead.

'And logic would suggest that the motive was the same,' Stella said softly.

I felt like crying again. But this time for a very different reason.

CHAPTER SIXTEEN

AFTER STELLA LEFT, I SAT staring at the wall for a long time. I felt cast adrift. I had put my life in Ben's hands more than once, and I'd covered his back as many times. For years, we'd been a team, always working with high stakes. I'd bounced my ideas off him. He'd been quick to find both the strong and the weak points in what I had to say. Together, we'd built cases against some of the worst villains this country has ever seen. Together, we'd put them behind bars for a very long time.

Of course we'd had our failures. Jack Farrell wasn't the only cleanskin walking the streets. But I'd always thought we had failed in spite of giving it our best shot. Now it looked as if the reason some cases had gone down the pan was the one every cop dreads. It seemed they'd gone tits-up not because we'd messed up but because my trusted partner had gone bent on me.

It hurt me both as a cop and as a man. I

thought I was a good judge of people. I'd always believed that I'd know in my gut if one of my team was crooked. It had never crossed my mind to doubt Ben. He was, I was sure, an honest cop. But more than that, he was my friend.

We'd been drunk together, crashed out together, sobered up together. We'd found the words and the trust to speak of the things men find it hardest to talk about – love, fear and need. I'd made excuses for him to his wife Karen. I'd eaten Sunday lunch at their table. I was godfather to his son Owen. And never once had I had any reason to wonder whether he was sincere.

And even in the face of what Stella had told me, it was a struggle to think the worst of him now. I kept trying to find another way to explain what Stella had found. The only thing I could come up with was the notion that Ben had been honest after all, and that Farrell had killed him because he knew Ben's death would throw us into a state of chaos and make us take our eyes off the ball with the other murders.

Even to myself, that sounded thin. Farrell had no reason to suspect we doubted the truth of his death, so he had no need of a red herring. And killing a cop was a hell of a red herring. Farrell was smart. He had to know that the murder of a policeman would send us into a frenzy. Killing Ben as a way of shifting our focus was well over the top.

No. Hard though it was for me to accept it, Stella's logic had the feel of something right on the money. It also explained why the fire had been set. It was partly to make sure the body was found without any delay. But it was also a way of linking Ben's murder to Katie Farrell.

As that thought crossed my mind, I felt an icy chill in my guts. What if the link was even stronger? What if the fire was sending a clearer message? What if it had been Ben himself who had set the fire that had killed Katie?

My stomach turned over at the very idea. Being a good dad was so much a part of who Ben had been. Of course, the other side of that was that he'd understand very clearly how much havoc Katie's death would wreak in Farrell. I still couldn't work out why, though. OK, Ben had always been pushy as a cop. He wanted to climb the greasy pole and he wanted to do it fast. There was no reason why it shouldn't be the same with him on the other side of the law. Maybe he'd thought the time was right to make his move.

But he wasn't in a position to run a major criminal empire like Farrell's. The only thing I could think of was that he'd been Farrell's man on the inside. And he'd ended up pushing Farrell hard for some reason or another, and Farrell had threatened his wife and kids. It could have been something as low level as, 'I know where you live.' But it would have been enough to send Ben over the edge in defence of his kids.

I groaned out loud. This was the very time when I would have turned to Ben to run my ideas past him. But now there was nobody. It wasn't that I doubted anyone else in the team, though if Ben was hooky, nobody was secure. No, it was simply that with Ben out of the picture, there was nobody who knew the way my mind worked.

Nobody apart from Stella, that is. But Stella's not a cop. She's the best at what she does, but she doesn't pretend to know how my job works. No, I was on my own with this one. I had to work it out for myself.

Time would be one way of testing this crazy

idea. If more villains died, then this was simply a gang war, the strong taking out the weak to make their point. But if it stopped here, then something different was going on.

But 'wait and see' isn't the best way to fight crime. You can solve things by sitting on your hands, but a lot of bad things tend to happen along the way before you get to the answer. And I'd already had enough bad shit to deal with in the past few weeks.

I forced myself to sit up and start making notes. My first thought was to drag Fancy Riley and Danny Chu off the streets and sweat them. I dumped the idea almost as soon as I had it. If they were in touch with the living Jack, I didn't want to tip him off that we knew he was alive and kicking. I could bring them in and question them about the murders, but I knew they wouldn't crack and there didn't seem much point.

I got up and pulled open my office door. 'Kirsty,' I shouted. Detective Constable Blythe looked up from her computer, startled.

'Sir?' she said, scrambling to her feet.

'Find out who did Jack Farrell's tattoos and bring him in,' I said.

Taking a single step made me feel better. The tattoo artist might be a dead end. But at least I was moving.

The next step was staring me in the face. A baby cop in his first day on the job would have worked it out. But I didn't want to take it. I didn't want to walk in on the grieving widow and start tearing her house apart.

But somebody was going to have to do it. And, like they say, better the devil you know.

CHAPTER SEVENTEEN

KAREN STILL LOOKED LIKE someone had ripped her heart out and handed it to her on a plate. Like it was a mistake she was still walking around, because how could she be doing anything at all when she was dead inside? I've seen that look before on the faces of the ones left behind after violent death. But this touched me like never before, because I cared for Karen and I had cared for the person she was mourning.

When Karen opened the door, there was a tragic flash of hope in her eyes, as if my being there might mean there had been some awful mistake and her Ben was really all right. But one look at my face and she knew there was no getting off this hook.

She fell into my arms and shivered, as if I'd brought cold air in with me. I held her close. 'I still feel gutted too,' I said, patting her back. But my eyes were looking around me with fresh wisdom. In the past, when I had said anything nice about the house or its contents, Ben had always made a big deal out of what a great bargain hunter Karen was. I'd taken it at face value. I had never stopped to wonder how they could afford to live with quite so much style on a sergeant's pay.

But looking at it coldly, not through the eyes of trust, it did seem like more than good taste and good shopping sense could provide. Not to mention the fact that no amount of skilled money-juggling could stretch his salary to a four-bedroomed house in the comfy end of Ealing. At the time he'd bought it, I'd accepted his story about a bequest from his mother's sister. As if! People like us don't have wealthy relations. But he said she'd come up on the pools, and I believed him. Because I wanted to, I suppose.

'I still can't take it in, Andy,' she said. Her voice was hoarse, like she'd been shouting too loud too long. 'Married to a cop, it's what you always fear. But the years go by and it never happens and you start to believe maybe it won't.'

'I know. It still seems unreal.' I steered her

into the living room and sat her down. 'Where are the kids?' I sat down beside her.

'They've been at my mum's. They don't need to see me like this.' She sniffed. 'What actually happened to him, Andy? Nobody will tell me and that makes me think the worst.'

I didn't know what to say. The truth wasn't even an option. 'He was stabbed, Karen. We're not even sure what he was doing down Paddington Basin. He must have been following a lead or meeting a snout. Something last-minute, because he hadn't told me about it.'

'Did he suffer?'

They always want to know that. Me, I've never thought that was the important thing. Being dead, that's the only bit that counts. 'Not for long, love.' I turned so I was facing her. 'Karen, I know Ben will have told you that the most important source of info in a murder case is the victim. So please don't think I'm being a heartless bastard when I say I've got to go through Ben's things.'

Karen frowned. 'What do you mean, his things? What's that got to do with him being dead?'

93

'Probably nothing. But we're not making as much progress as I'd like. And as I said, we don't know why he was there or who he was meeting. There's nothing in his desk to give us a clue. So I need to take a look in his study, see if there's anything there.'

Karen folded her arms across her chest, drawing away from me. 'Why would he have it at home? He kept his work at the office.'

I spread my hands in a helpless gesture. 'You know what he was like. He wanted to get on. I wouldn't put it past him to be working on something he'd kept up his sleeve, so he could surprise me with it. It wouldn't be the first time.' It was the truth, though now I saw it through different eyes.

'Plus, we're all a bit paranoid on our squad,' I added. 'The kind of villains we turn over can afford to buy a copper or two. Not on our team, naturally – that goes without saying. But from time to time, the odd spy tries to sneak under our radar. So we all tend to be a bit careful with anything that's really sensitive.' I gave her my best 'trust me' look. 'The only thing I care about is nailing the bastard who did this.'

She was still keeping her distance, but she

looked less upset. I felt like a complete bastard, laying on the bullshit like that. But I had to know. Karen held her face in her hands and shook her head. 'I'm sorry, Andy. I'm not thinking straight. I know you're not going to rest till you've got him. Go on through.' She nodded towards the hall.

I leaned forward and gave her an awkward hug, then got up and headed for the boxroom out by the garage. It was a nice little space, about ten feet by eight, with a shallow frosted window that ran along the top of the outside wall. Andy had it kitted out with a black wooden desk, a leather chair, a state-of-the-art computer, a TV and a PlayStation. The desk drawers were all unlocked. They shouted, *Look, I'm a man with nothing to hide.*

It seemed like they were telling the truth. I went through every scrap of paper and there was nothing there that wasn't blameless. Stuff to do with the house, the car, the top-of-the-range goodies the house was crammed with. Bank statements that looked exactly as they should.

I was getting brassed off. I knew there had to be more somewhere. All my instincts were on red alert now. The study was like a stage set. It was too perfect, too blameless. I could feel Ben thumbing his nose at me.

The bottom drawer held all the personal stuff. Passport, birth certificate, national health card, his will. More out of frustration than anything else, I pulled it out and unfolded it. I started reading, not expecting any surprises. About halfway through came a short sentence that stopped me in my tracks. My heart sank and soared in the same moment.

Bingo.

CHAPTER EIGHTEEN

KAREN'S FROWN BECAME DEEPER as she read the will. 'What does that mean?' she said, her red-rimmed eyes looking puzzled.

'You inherit the lot,' I said. 'The will lists the main things. But it also says that you get anything else Ben owned, even if it isn't laid out in so many words.'

'Yeah, I got that,' Karen said. 'But why are the contents of his health club locker listed? Ben didn't belong to a health club. He worked out at the police gym. He said health clubs were for wankers who wanted to pretend they were fit.'

'That's what I wondered.' Because I also knew Ben's views about health clubs. And this wasn't just any health club. It was Smithson's. The place where Jack Farrell had gone every morning with Danny Chu and Fancy Riley. And where, apparently, Ben Wilson had had a locker. I sighed. 'I need to check this out, Karen.'

She frowned again. 'You think that was where he put the things he wanted to keep secure?'

'It's possible. I'm going to need a note from you saying it's OK for me to look in the locker, though.' I hoped she was so dazed she'd agree. I knew I didn't have enough for a search warrant.

I was in luck. 'Anything I can do to help.' Karen got to her feet and cast around for something to write on. In the end, I knocked something out on Ben's computer and got her to sign it.

Just over an hour later, I was in the manager's office at Smithson's. It was better furnished than the living rooms of most of the cops I know. Lavish was clearly what they were aiming for, and they'd hit the target. The manager was a hawk-faced man in his thirties. I'd seen him before, in photos we'd snatched of Jack Farrell enjoying the high life at the health club. But he wasn't smiling at me the way he smiled at Farrell. 'This all seems a bit –'

'Out of the usual run of things? I couldn't agree more,' I said. 'But you know how it is when a cop is killed. We're desperate to cover all the bases.' I gave him the quick snake smile that doesn't get as far as my eyes. 'I hope you're not going to create a problem here? I do have his widow's go-ahead, and a copy of the will where he mentions the locker by number.'

He rolled his eyes. 'Can we at least be discreet about this?'

I looked innocent. 'That's why I'm here alone. I could have come mob-handed, you know.'

'You've got the combination?' he said with ill grace.

I pointed to the will. 'Right there.'

He took me down to the locker room, an annex off the changing rooms with a bench running between two banks of locked doors. He pointed out Ben's locker, then hung around behind me. 'Thank you,' I said. 'I'll manage by myself now.' He wasn't happy about it, but he took the hint.

The locker was on the floor level. It was about thirty inches by twelve and when I opened it, most of the space was taken up by a sports holdall. I pulled it out, grunting at the unexpected weight of it. I laid it on the bench and unzipped it.

If I'd had any doubts about where Stella's

logic had taken us, they died then. Ben hadn't sold himself cheaply, that was for sure. The bag was rammed with bundles of fifty-pound notes. I had no idea how much was there, but it must have run well into six figures. 'You bastard,' I said.

The betrayal didn't end there. The locker also held a couple of envelopes. One was labelled *Insurance*. It contained one of those life insurance policies with a big single premium and a huge payout. This one had been taken out a couple of years before and it would pay half a million pounds, all to Karen. I couldn't believe how long this had been going on. A couple of years ago, he'd had fifty grand to blow on insurance. All the while complaining to me that he could barely afford to insure his bloody car.

I thought that was bad enough. But there was worse to come. The second envelope was addressed to Karen. I didn't think twice. I ripped it open.

My darling Karen,
If you're reading this, it's because I'm dead.
I'm sorry for leaving you and the kids behind.
All I ever wanted was to spend the rest of our

lives together. But at least I can make sure that, even if you don't have me, you will have enough money never to need to worry about making ends meet.

I know you must be wondering where all this cash has come from. I'm not proud of this, but a while back, Andy and I turned over a big villain up in the Midlands. The guy got blown away by one of his own sidekicks. He always kept huge amounts of cash on the premises. I suppose we should have handed it in, but only the two of us knew about it, and it seemed too good to miss. It was Andy's idea, but I didn't try very hard to talk him out of it. So we decided to keep our mouths shut and split it between us. I bought the insurance policy with some of the money and the rest of it is in the bag.

I know you will be tempted to do what feels like the right thing and dob me in. I beg you not to do that if Andy's still alive. For his sake, and for the sake of the kids, keep quiet and make the most of what I've been able to provide. I don't want my kids to grow up thinking I was a bad man. I'm not a bad man, Karen. I just gave in to the chance to get my hands on some real dosh. I wasn't hurting anybody and I don't want you to hurt Andy or the kids by coming clean now about what I did.

Karen, I've loved you from the day I met you. I will be looking over your shoulder every day for the rest of your life, watching over you and keeping you safe. You were the only woman for me.

All my love, your Ben

'You bastard,' I said again. With his fake account of where the money had come from, he'd slid out from under any link to Jack Farrell or any other criminal stuff.. And he'd pointed the finger straight at me. I couldn't hand this in, not without spending the rest of my career as the subject of whispers and gossip about my honesty.

And I'd thought he was my friend. I felt an ache inside me, the kind you get when you've held back your tears for too long.

It wasn't Ben's death that was making me feel so bad.

It was what he'd done with his life.

CHAPTER NINETEEN

THERE WAS GOOD NEWS and bad news waiting for me when I got back to the office. Kirsty Blythe had returned with the news that John 'Pirate' Hawkins, the tattoo artist who had done Jack Farrell's tattoos, had been reported missing by his girlfriend the day before the fake suicide. He was still on the missing list.

The good news was that Manuela the Spanish nanny wasn't as clever about covering her tracks as Farrell. I'd had an alert put out on her credit card after she'd skipped the country. It had paid off. According to the report on my desk, she had used the card to buy a load of groceries, toiletries and clothes in a hyper-market on the outskirts of Calais.

Things were starting to fall into place. We knew Farrell had been using his boat as a base for making the deals when he'd been selling up, and that Fancy Riley had taken him off on a speedboat at the end of every day. That would make sense if Farrell had a second boat that we knew nothing about. It would also explain why there had been no sightings of him. If he was using his boat to move between England and France, he could come and go more or less as he pleased. He could come here to torture and kill, then slip back to France the same night.

It didn't narrow things down much, but it was a start. That evening, sitting at Stella's dining table and working my way through a Chinese banquet, I brought her up to speed. I could see she was shaken by the depth of the sleaze Ben had crawled into. 'What did you do with the money?' she said.

I gave her a quick look out of the corner of my eye. 'I gave Karen the insurance policy,' I said. 'I burned the letter. And the money's sitting in my car.'

'What are you going to do with it?' Stella put down her chopsticks and gave me a stern look.

'Give it away,' I said. 'Where it'll do some good.' I took a gulp of wine. 'Karen's got more than enough.'

Stella reached across and covered my hand with hers. 'Don't beat yourself up, Andy. What Ben did, it's not your fault.'

'I should have seen it. I should have known,' I said, a bitter taste in my mouth that had nothing to do with the food. 'He was my right hand, and I didn't know he was dirty. How can I call myself a cop when I let that happen?'

'He chose which way to go. He chose to turn his whole life into a lie,' Stella said. 'I won't sit back and let you blame yourself for that.'

'I'm not blaming myself for his choice, I'm blaming myself for trusting a man who didn't deserve it.'

Stella squeezed my hand. 'You're right about that, at least. But he must have worked very hard to make you trust him. He must have been scared shitless that you would find him out. And, frankly, he deserved every second of that fear. You're a good man, Andy. And a good cop.'

I snorted. 'I don't think so, Stella. Ben fooled me. Jack Farrell's still fooling me. He might be in France. He might be at sea.' I drank more wine. 'He might be sitting outside your flat laughing at us, for all I know.'

'Why France?'

I told her about Manuela and the credit card. Stella let go of my hand and stood up. 'I've got an idea,' she said. It must have been a good one. She was walking away from one of the best Chinese takeaways in London.

I followed her through to the space under the stairs that she'd converted into a study. She sat down at the computer, which she left running twenty-four seven in spite of my warnings about ID theft and hackers. She made her way to a private site for forensic experts who specialize in figuring out ways to identify bodies. She glanced up at me. 'Could you get me my wine, please?'

By the time I got back, she was swapping instant messages with a colleague.

DrStel: That's right. Tattoo removal.
JPB: Laser or surgery?
DrStel: Doesn't matter. Any kind. What matters is where. Got to be Calais area.
JPB: Gimme 5.

'Who's JPB?' I asked, setting her drink down beside the keyboard.

She took a sip then said, 'A skin man in Paris. I worked with him in Kosovo. He's the one who taught me about tattoos.' Before she could say more, the computer beeped. JPB had come up with a couple of addresses of clinics in the right area.

JPB: The one in Calais is more of a general clinic. The other is more expert with tattoo work. I met the clinic director in Geneva, he was talking about a new cream they were using with the lasers to give a better result. This cream is their own formula. He thinks it will make them rich once they have proved how well it works. If I was having my tattoos removed in the north of France, I think this is where I would go.
DrStel: Thanks, Jean-Paul. I'll buy you a drink at EUBIC next month.

Stella looked up at me with a grin. 'I wondered why Manuela was in France. It didn't seem to make sense unless she was there for Farrell. Which begged the question, why Calais? There are so many little places along the French coast where there would be much less chance of Farrell being spotted. There had to be a good reason.'

I grinned. 'Like, getting rid of a unique set of

tattoos. Stella, you're a better detective than me.' I leaned down and kissed her. 'But you're also your own worst enemy. I'm going to have to go now and talk to the team about what we do next.'

'Andy,' she howled. 'Surely it can wait till morning?'

I held my hands up, fending her off. 'I'm not taking any chances,' I said, backing towards the front door. 'Save me some dinner in case I make it back later.'

I should have taken Stella's idea straight to my boss and let him liaise with the French. But Jack Farrell was mine and I didn't want him slipping through the net because some French cop who didn't care enough was having a power nap at the wrong minute.

I hand-picked four officers, and we went off to France on the Eurostar. Once we were there, we hired three cars. We started staking out the clinic in four-hour shifts, holing up between times in a lorry drivers' motel off the nearby motorway.

I had plenty of time to think about Katie Farrell's murder. It had been more than a week since Ben had died, and there hadn't been any more bodies. Plus his was the only murder marked out with a fire. To me, it seemed clear. Jack Farrell had tortured and murdered his way to the answer. Then he had sent a message to the rest of us with the fire that linked Ben's death to Katie's. Only a dad who loved his kids like Ben would know how much damage Katie's murder would do. I didn't know why he'd done it, but all my instincts as a cop said that he had.

On the third day, we got lucky. Kirsty Blythe and her partner spotted Manuela dropping Farrell off at the side door of the clinic just before seven in the morning. She picked him up again two hours later. By then, all five of us were in place for a perfect tail.

First we followed them to a private marina where they loaded some hypermarket plastic bags on board a good-sized floating gin palace. We couldn't get inside without keys, but I got out the binoculars and made sure I knew which boat.

Then we followed them about twenty miles into the countryside. There was no chance of losing them on the long flat straight roads lined with poplars. They pulled in at a large modern villa on the far edge of a smart little village that looked like a movie set. After they'd taken the rest of the shopping inside, we carried on a few miles to the next village where we celebrated quietly with beers all round.

'That villa's a bitch to stake out,' Blythe said.

'We don't need to stake it out. There's only one road through the village. We just need to split ourselves up. Two cars to the north, one to the south. We'll pick them up when they leave.'

Nobody had a better idea. It meant we were more or less trapped with the vehicles, but it could have been worse. And luckily, it didn't go on very long.

Just before midnight that night, the first car on the road north called in to say Farrell had just driven past, alone and pedal to the metal. Blythe and I swung straight out into the road and kept a steady speed till we saw headlights behind us. We picked up our pace so he wouldn't overtake us too soon and to give the others a chance to catch up.

There were a couple of hairy moments, but we managed to keep on his tail all the way to the marina car park. As Farrell walked towards the gate, we made our move, screeching the cars to a halt around him, jumping out and taking him down. It took four of us to subdue him, but he never really stood a chance.

We cuffed him, took his keys off him and marched him to his boat while Kirsty parked the cars up neatly and left the keys under the drivers' seats. We'd call the rental company when we got home.

The main reason I'd chosen Kirsty came to the fore now. She could sail. She'd been messing around on boats since she was a kid and she'd been crisscrossing the Channel on her parents' little cabin cruiser for as long as she could remember.

We stuck Farrell below in the main bedroom, while those of us who weren't driving sat in the saloon and played cards. Farrell kept up a steady stream of swearing and shouting for a while, but he got tired of it before we did.

We were back on English soil in time for breakfast. The story was simple. We'd had a tip that Farrell was on his way back and we'd caught him as he stepped ashore. His word against five of ours. No contest.

At first, it looked like there wasn't much we could charge him with. Faking a suicide isn't that big a deal. But thanks to Stella, that soon changed. She got an ID for the body we'd mistaken for Farrell. The guy worked in Farrell's porn business and he'd last been seen leaving a bar with Fancy Riley and Farrell himself. That was good, but even better was the discovery of the knife that had killed Brian Cooper and Ben Wilson. It was in the cutlery drawer on Farrell's boat, his prints all over it. The final nail in the coffin was the experts matching traces of explosive in a locker on the boat to the stuff that had blown Joey Scardino to bits.

It's been almost a year since the night Katie Farrell died. Her father's due to stand trial in a few weeks. Funny how many rats came out of the woodwork to lay stuff at his door once they knew we had him bang to rights on something major.

It's been a long journey for all of us. Karen Wilson's still adrift in grief and her kids look like lost souls. We kept Ben's name clean and I think that'll survive the trial. But I feel like I've paid a high price for that. After Ben, I can't find it in me to trust anyone. Something I couldn't hide from Stella. She left for Knoxville, Tennessee and the Body Farm a couple of weeks ago. As far as I can see, the only winners have been a bunch of charities that help homeless kids, drug addicts and women sold into sexual slavery.

Like I said, when a child dies, everybody hurts. And some hurts can't ever be healed.

WORLD BOOK DAY
Quick Reads

Quick Reads are published alongside and in partnership with BBC RaW.

We would like to thank all our partners in the *Quick* Reads project for all their help and support:

Department for Education and Skills
Trades Union Congress
The Vital Link
The Reading Agency
National Literacy Trust

Quick Reads would also like to thank the Arts Council England and National Book Tokens for their sponsorship.

We would also like to thank the following companies for providing their services free of charge: SX Composing for typesetting all the titles; Icon Reproduction for text reproduction; Norske Skog, Stora Enso, PMS and Iggusend for paper/board supplies; Mackays of Chatham, Cox and Wyman, Bookmarque, White Quill Press, Concise, Norhaven and GGP for the printing.

www.worldbookday.com

Quick Reads

BOOKS IN THE *Quick* Reads SERIES

Look out for more titles in the *Quick* Reads series being published in 2007.

www.worldbookday.com

Have you enjoyed reading this
Quick Reads **book?**

Would you like to read more?

Or learn how to write fantastically?

If so, you might like to attend a course to
develop your skills.

Courses are **free** and available in your local area.

If you'd like to find out more,
phone **0800 100 900**.

You can also ask for a **free video or DVD** showing
other people who have been on our courses and
the changes they have made in their lives.

Don't get by – get on.

FIRST CHOICE BOOKS

If you enjoyed this book, you'll find more great reads on www.firstchoicebooks.org.uk. First Choice Books allows you to search by type of book, author and title. So, whether you're looking for romance, sport, humour – or whatever turns you on – you'll be able to find other books you'll enjoy.

You can also borrow books from your local library. If you tell them what you've enjoyed, they can recommend other good reads they think you will like.

First Choice is part of The Vital Link, promoting reading for pleasure. To find out more about The Vital Link visit www.vitallink.org.uk

RaW

BBC RaW is the BBC's biggest-ever campaign about reading and writing. Find out more online at bbc.co.uk/raw or telephone 08000 150 950.

NEW ISLAND

New Island publishers have produced four series of books in its Open Door series – brilliant short novels for adults from the cream of Irish writers. Visit www.newisland.ie and go to the Open Door section.

SANDSTONE PRESS

In the Sandstone Vista Series, Sandstone Press Ltd publish quality contemporary fiction and non-fiction books. The full list can be found at their website www.sandstonepress.com.

Quick Reads

The Dying Wish by Courttia Newland

Abacus

How do you want to be remembered?

Private investigator Ervine James is feeling great. Business is booming, and his new partner Carmen Sinclair is smarter and sharper than he could ever have hoped. But then, by chance, he meets a woman with strange eyes, and the company in the office next door mysteriously disappears. Soon Ervine is drawn into a puzzle so deep, so sinister, that the truth could cost him his life.

Quick Reads

Desert Claw by Damien Lewis

Arrow

In present-day Iraq thieves roam the streets. People are being killed in broad daylight. Security is non-existent. And now, terrorists have seized a Van Gogh painting worth £25 million from one of Saddam's palaces. They are offering it to the highest bidder . . .

Mick Kilbride and his buddy 'East End' Eddie are ex-SAS soldiers. The British Government doesn't want to pay the ransom money to the terrorists. Instead, it hires Mick and his team of ex-Special Forces to get the painting back. Their mission takes them into a dark and violent world where all is not as it seems. And if Mick and Eddie are going to stay alive, they're going to have to stay one step ahead of the enemy . . . and their betrayers.

Quick Reads

The Grey Man by Andy McNab

Corgi

Kevin Dodds leads a dull, uneventful life. He has a steady job at the bank, a nice house and car. His wife goes to bingo on a Saturday night, but he usually stays in to save money.

But one Saturday Kevin decides he'd like a night out himself. And he's not talking about a pint and a packet of peanuts down at the local. He's going to attempt to pull off one of the biggest bank robberies in history.

The priceless 'Augusta' necklace is being held in the safe of the bank where Kevin works. Armed only with information gleaned from the web, a Margaret Thatcher mask and climbing equipment he doesn't really know how to use, Kevin is about to take a heart-thumping step into the unknown. For once, he's going to stop being the grey man

Quick Reads

Danny Wallace and the Centre of the Universe
by Danny Wallace

Ebury

Danny Wallace wanted to write about the Centre of the Universe, but how was he to get there? And what would he say about it when he did?

Luckily, in a small street, in a small town in Idaho, a manhole cover had just been declared the Centre of the Universe by the mayor. The science backed his decision and the town rejoiced.

And the name of the town? Wallace. It was a cosmic coincidence Danny couldn't resist . . .

Quick Reads

The Name You Once Gave Me
by Mike Phillips

HarperCollins

Daniel's getting married next week. He's got his future all worked out. It's his past that's the problem.

Daniel never knew his father. All his mother would tell him was that his dad had been a Nigerian who had died before Daniel was born. He didn't even know what his dad looked like until an old neighbour showed him a picture.

But the man in the photo is still alive . . . and now Daniel will stop at nothing to find him.